Dr. Roach

ISBN 978-0-545-42557-5

Text copyright © 2012 Boxer Books Limited. Written by Paul Harrison. Illustrations copyright © 2012 by Tom Knight.

First published in Great Britain in 2012 by Boxer Books Limited. Based on an original idea by Sam Williams. Monstrous Stories™ concept, names, stories, designs, and logos © 2012 Boxer Books Limited.

12 11 10 9 8 7 6 5 4 3 2 1   13 14 15 16 17 18/0

Printed in the U.S.A.   40
First Scholastic printing, April 2013

The display type was set in Adobe Garamond.
The text type was set in Blackmoor Plain and Adobe Casion.
Book design by Nina Goffi

DR. ROACH'S
M🪳NSTROUS STORIES

THE DAY THE MICE STOOD STILL

SCHOLASTIC INC.

Contents

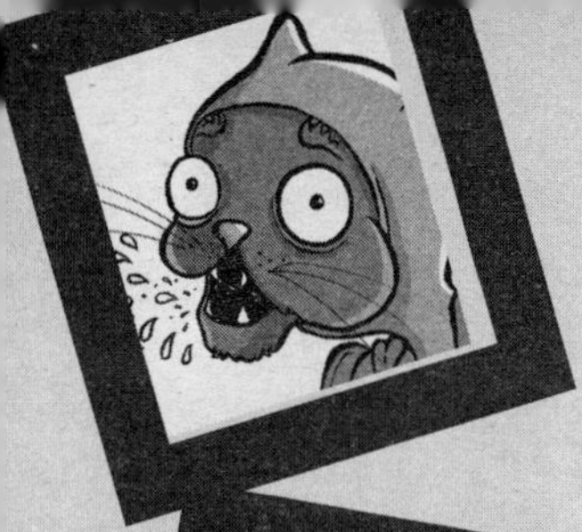

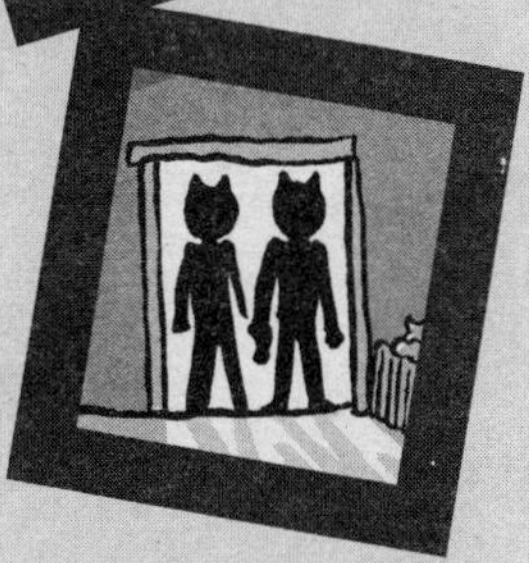

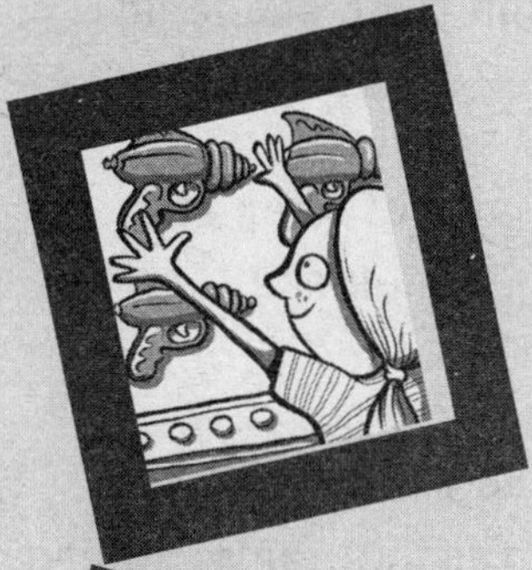

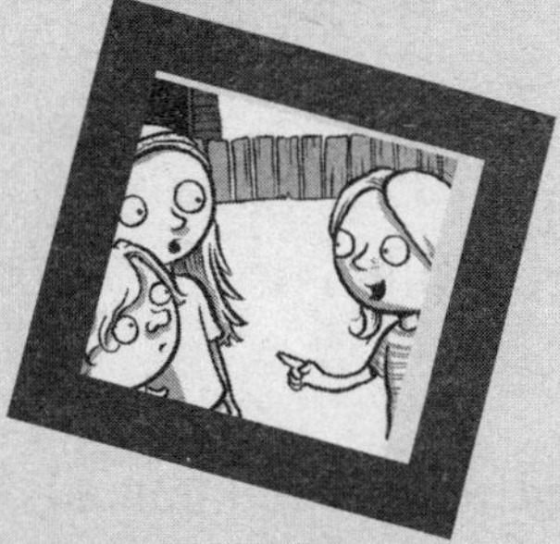

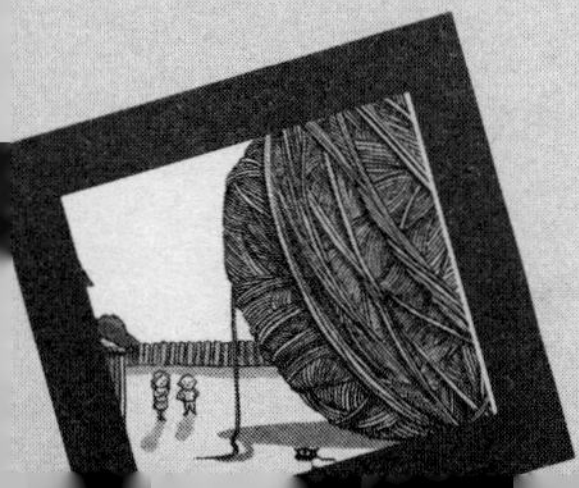

Dr. Roach Welcomes YOU!

What can make all the mice in a small town suddenly stand still? A piece of giant cheese? A huge mousetrap?

No, it's a flying saucer from outer space! Alien cats have come to Earth. These talking tabbies say they've come to help take care of the town's mouse problem.

But Jilly McCafferty is worried. The mice aren't the only things disappearing from her family's farm. So are their cows!

Could the feline visitors be cow-nappers? Is their friendly act just a big purr-formance? Jilly is determined to solve this mystery.

How you ask? Come closer, my friend, and I'll tell you all about it.

Welcome to Dr. Roach's Monstrous Stories. Enjoy!

Dr. Roach

"Eeeeeeeekkkkkkkk!"

Jilly McCafferty sat straight up in bed. Was that a scream?

"Eeeeeeeeekkkkkkk!"

Yep, that was a scream all right, and it came from the kitchen. Jilly leaped out of bed like a dog at breakfast and raced into the room. Her mother was there, perched on a chair, her knees knocking so hard with fear that the chair was rattling across the floor like a crab in a hurry.

"Mom, what's wrong?" she asked.

"M-m-m-m-mouse," she stammered, pointing to the corner of the room.

"Oh, Mom, get a grip, we live on a farm! You should be used to mice by now!" said Jilly, walking over to where the mouse was. "Look, it's friendly. It's not even running away."

The mouse was standing perfectly still. Jilly got closer and closer and still the mouse stood there. Jilly went right up to it and touched it.

"I think it's dead," she said. "No, it's still breathing, but it's like it's frozen stiff. Weird."

Mrs. McCafferty got down from her chair and nervously edged over.

"Well, it's still horrible. Put it outside, and then you'd better get ready for school."

Jilly scooped up the mouse, but she had no intention of just leaving it outside. Nothing exciting ever happened in Buffalo Bottom, the

town where Jilly lived. It was tiny and mostly made up of small farms. This was the best thing to have happened in a long time.

"You, my furry friend, are coming to school," she whispered as she slipped the rigid rodent into her school bag.

Chapter 2
Stiff Mice

The doors to the school bus were barely open before Jilly had leaped on. She quickly found her best friend, Rod, and plopped down on the seat next to him.

"Rod — you're not going to believe this!" said Jilly. Proudly, she lifted the mouse out of her bag.

"I bet you've never seen anything like this bef . . ." Her words faded away. Rod was holding a stiff mouse exactly like hers.

"And we're not the only ones," said Rod. "Show her, everyone."

All over the bus, the school kids held up boxes and bags with frozen

mice in them. Everywhere Jilly looked there were mice: in backpacks, in the pockets of the seats, even one on the dashboard of the bus.

"There were mice everywhere," Jilly told her mom that evening.

"Ooh, I know, I've never seen so many. I've been finding them around the farm all day. Disgusting!" Mrs. McCafferty replied. "Anyway, young lady, it's time for bed."

Reluctantly, Jilly made her way upstairs. It took her forever to get to sleep. This mice thing was just too weird. Eventually, she tried counting them. They worked as well as sheep, and soon she was fast asleep.

*Eeeeeeeeeeeeeeeyyyyyyyyyyyyyy
oooooowwwwwwww!*

Jilly woke up with a start and sat straight up. The house was filled with bright light. What on earth was that? There was something in the yard.

"Mom!"

Chapter 3
Flying Saucer

Jilly rushed out of her room and ran straight into her mom.

"What's happening?" asked her mom.

"There's only one way to find out," said Jilly. "Come on."

Jilly grabbed her mother's hand and dragged her out of the house.

"I'm not sure this is a good idea," her mom protested. "It could be anything out there . . . we're not expecting visitors."

But, expected or not, visitors they had. A large, silver, saucer-shaped spaceship had landed in the farmyard. Lights flashed around the middle of

the craft, and small clouds of steam burst from flaps here and there.

"It's, it's, it's . . ." Mrs. McCafferty stammered.

"A spaceship!" said Jilly.

"I'm calling the police!" said Mrs. McCafferty, running into the house.

"I'm calling Rod!" said Jilly, running for her phone.

Within the hour, Jilly's farm was filled with curious people from Buffalo Bottom all watching the spaceship and waiting for something to happen.

HHHIIIIIIIISSSSSSSSSSSSS!

A door opened, and a ramp was lowered to the ground.

The light from inside the spaceship was so bright it was impossible to see properly. The outline of a tall figure appeared and began to descend the steps. It seemed to be wearing a cape and had what looked like two points on the top of its head.

"Is it the two-pointy-headed monster from Jupiter?" cried one of the townsfolk.

"Is it the alien vampire from Mars?" shouted another.

The figure moved out of the blinding light, and the crowd saw it clearly.

"No, it's a cat!" said Jilly.

Chapter 4
Alien Fur Ball

The cat was taller than the tallest human, walking on its hind legs and wearing a silver cape. It held up a paw to silence the crowd.

"*Heuwww! Heuwwwwww!*" said the cat alien.

"Uh, sorry?" said Rod.

"Maybe it can't breathe our air and it's choking," said Mrs. McCafferty.

"*Heuwww! Heuwww! Ptah!*" The alien cat spat out a large hairball.

"*Euuuurrrgggh!*" said the crowd.

"Sorry about that," the cat replied in a silky voice. "My name is Felix Andromedus. I come from the planet Felinus. My crew and I come in peace. Take me to your milk. . . . I mean, take me to your leader."

The mayor was pushed to the front of the crowd.

"Leader of the Earth people," began the cat.

"I don't lead all the people of Earth," the mayor said.

"Ah, of course, you must be the president of the U.S.A. then," the cat replied.

"Mayor," the mayor explained, "of Buffalo Bottom."

The cat looked like it was struggling to understand.

"Very well. President Mayor's Bottom, we have been monitoring your planet, and we have detected your mouse problem.

We have a proposal for you. We shall rid you of these mice in return for . . . milk!"

"Well, that seems like an excellent idea. On behalf of the good people of Buffalo Bottom, I accept," said the mayor.

Chapter 5
Lost Cows

The next few days were very exciting.
No one ever visited Buffalo Bottom,
but now there were giant cat aliens all
over town. Apart from the occasional
hairball, they were good to have
around. And being cats, they were
very tidy. Plus, the mice were gone.

But that wasn't the only thing going missing. There were problems at the McCafferty farm, and Jilly was worried.

"What's wrong?" Rod asked Jilly on the way to school.

"We've lost some cows," said Jilly.

"Cows are huge. How can you lose

one of them?"
asked Rod.

"I reckon those
cats have got
something to
do with it," Jilly

replied. "Something isn't right, and
it only started when they arrived
in town."

"People always blame strangers when things go wrong," said Rod. "I mean, where would the aliens keep cows?"

Jilly didn't know, but as sure as cats like milk, she was going to find out.

That night, Jilly hid herself in the cow barn and waited. She was just beginning to fall asleep when she heard noises.

"Cats!" whispered Jilly to herself. "What are they up to?"

"This is too easy!" laughed one of the cats.

"Humans! They'll believe anything! Even the mice knew we were coming.

They froze stiff out of fear! And rightly so!" said the other cat.

He pointed a ray gun at a cow.

BAZAM!

A beam of light shot out. The cow glowed and then shrunk to the size of a mouse.

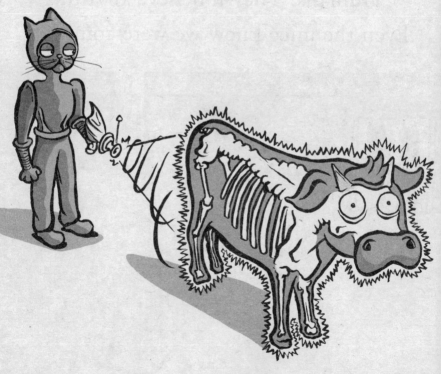

"Once we're home on Felinus, a simple blast of the gun and the cows are back to full size. Then we'll have all the milk we want!"

"And we leave tonight, so we need to shrink them all."

And they laughed their terrible alien cat laugh:

"*Meow-how-how, meow-how-how, meow-how-how!*"

Chapter 6
Ray Guns

The cats shrank the rest of the cows and carried them off to the spaceship.

"I've got to get in there and rescue those cows!" said Jilly.

There was no one on the ramp into the spaceship, so Jilly took her chance and sprinted over to it. A quick peek up the ramp — all clear.

"Well, it's now or never," muttered Jilly, and she crept inside as quickly as she could. The ship was bright, shiny, and very, very clean. Jilly slipped down the corridor and turned a corner. A cat! She ducked into a room before she was spotted and silently shut the door.

"*Moo*."

Jilly spun around. She was in a large room piled high with crates of milk, and full of tiny cows!

"Success!" whispered Jilly. "Now, what was it they said? Something about using the gun again. . . . I wonder if it's one of these?"

Jilly took a ray gun off the wall.

Then she emptied a crate of milk cartons and filled it with cows instead.

"And what do you think you're doing?"

Felix, the leader of the cats, stood in the doorway, with the rest of his crew behind him.

"Getting out of here!" said Jilly. She
pointed the ray gun at the cows.
"Stop her!" shouted Felix.

Too late.

MAZAB!

A blast of light
covered the cows.
The box shook,
then bulged,
then ripped
apart as the cows
got bigger and
bigger.

"Come on,
girls!" shouted Jilly.
"We're going home!"

Chapter 7
The Chase

The cows charged out of the room with Jilly close behind them. The cats were scattered this way and that.

Down the hall went the herd and down the ramp to freedom!

"What's all the noise?" asked Mrs. McCafferty, running into the yard.

"It's the aliens, Mom! They're trying to steal the cows. Get help!"

The cats, battered and bruised, rose unsteadily to their feet.

"She's taken our cows!" said one.

"Worse than that," said Felix, "look at the state of our spaceship!"

It was covered in cow poo.

Word spread quickly around Buffalo Bottom. Soon, a crowd

had gathered at the farm, just as the spaceship took off.

Eeeeeeeeeeeeeeeyyyyyyyyyyyy oooooowwwwwwwww!

It hovered above the McCaffertys' farm.

"President Mayor's Bottom, people of Earth, you have displeased us!" came

Felix's voice over the loudspeaker. "Prepare to be destroyed . . . as soon as we have tidied up in here. We shall be back!"

With that, the spaceship zoomed into space.

"Listen, everyone," shouted Jilly. "They might be super-advanced aliens, but they're still just cats. And we're not going to get beaten by a bunch of tabbies!"

"But what are we going to do?" asked the mayor.

"I've got a plan," Jilly replied. "Rod,

we're going to need all the sheep from your farm, and everyone else's farm, too. And Mom, get the crop-dusting plane ready for take-off. We're going to show these kitties who's boss!"

Chapter 8
Great Balls of Yarn

The good people of Buffalo Bottom worked through the night. They sheared the sheep and spun the wool. By daybreak they had a ball of yarn the size of a house. And just in time . . .

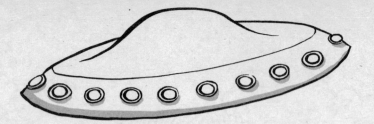

*Eeeeeeeeeeeeeeyyyyyyyyyyyy
oooooowwwwwwwww!*

"Puny earthlings," boomed Felix's voice, "prepare to meet your doo . . . hold on a minute, what's that? Oooohhhh, yarn!"

"Got them!" said Jilly to Rod. "Okay, tie the end to Mom's plane."

"Earthlings! Give us the yarn and we might spare your worthless lives!"

"Come and get it, fur ball!" said Jilly. She jumped into the passenger seat of her mother's crop-dusting plane. It was only an old-fashioned biplane, but Mrs. McCafferty was the best pilot in the state. The engine spluttered into life, and they were off, dragging the yarn ball into the air behind them.

"After them!" cried Felix.

"Okay, Mom," shouted Jilly over the noise of the engine, "you fly, I'll direct. Take a right into the canyon."

Zooooooom went the plane. *Eeeeeee yyyyyyyyyooooowwwwwww* went the spaceship, as it followed the plane around the rocky cliff faces of the canyon.

"Now left!" said Jilly.

Zooooooom.

Eeeeeeeyyyyyyyyyyooooowwwwww.

"Now right!"

Zooooooom.

Eeeeeeeyyyyyyyyyyooooowwwwww.

The spaceship was almost on top of them.

"Pull up, NOW!"
The nimble little biplane suddenly

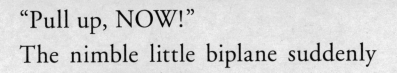

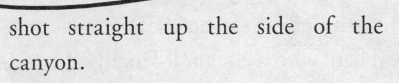

shot straight up the side of the canyon.

Zooooooom.

But the spaceship didn't!

Eeeeeeyyyyyyyyy C C C C R R R R AAAASSSSSHHHHHH!

The battered spaceship lay in
a crumpled heap on the ground.
Then, with a cough, it finally rose up,
rattling back up into the sky and
tearing off into outer space.

The biplane landed beside the
cheering townsfolk.

"I reckon that's the last we'll see of them," said Jilly.

"In a way, it's a shame they're gone. It was nice having visitors," said the mayor.

"And we'll have visitors again," said Rod, "now that Jilly's given us

our new tourist
attraction —
the world's
largest ball
of yarn!"

HURRY!

Meet Judd Crank and his friend Zak. Two ordinary boys, in an ordinary town, with some very ordinary goldfish.

Who would have thought that those ordinary goldfish would become great monsters and step right out of their tank and into town — looking for trouble?

How you ask? Get a copy today and I'll tell you everything!

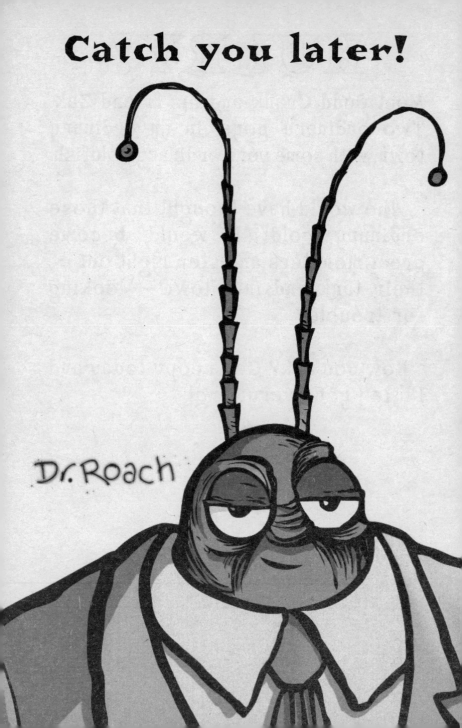